The Dragon's Dentist

There are lots of Early Reader stories
you might enjoy.

Look at the back of the book or,
for a complete list, visit
www.orionchildrensbooks.co.uk

The Dragon's Dentist

By John McLay

Illustrated by Martin Brown

Orion
Children's Books

ORION CHILDREN'S BOOKS

First published in Great Britain in 2014 by Orion Children's Books
This edition published in 2016 by Hodder and Stoughton

9 10 8

Text copyright © John McLay, 2014
Illustrations copyright © Martin Brown, 2014

The moral rights of the author and illustrator have been asserted.

A CIP catalogue record for this book
is available from the British Library.

ISBN 978 1 4440 1104 3

Printed and bound in China

The paper and board used in this book are
made from wood from responsible sources.

Orion Children's Books
An imprint of
Hachette Children's Group
Part of Hodder and Stoughton
Carmelite House
50 Victoria Embankment
London EC4Y 0DZ

An Hachette UK Company
www.hachette.co.uk

hachettechildrens.co.uk

To Charlie

Contents

Chapter One

Harry dreamed of knights.

His dad was a famous knight.
So was his big brother.
Even Harry's sister was a knight.

"I'm not even a knight-in-waiting," said Harry to his horse, Oats. Oats was quite big. He liked eating a lot of oats.

Harry's job was to look after the shields. He had to clean them in case they were needed for battles …

… Or for slaying dragons.

"I'm a very good cleaner of shields, Oats," said Harry, "but I want to be a knight." Harry wondered if he was too small to be a knight. Lots of girls were bigger than him.

Even Oats was taller. And a bit fatter. Harry was certainly the shortest member of his family.

"Why can't I be a knight, Oats?"
asked Harry. "I'm brave."

"I'm clever."

"I'm strong."

"I'm even good with animals."

Harry was not happy.

Chapter Two

One morning, Harry sat cleaning the shields after a very muddy battle.

He decided to prove he could be a great knight. He decided to capture Eric.

Eric the Viking who raided
castles and stole gold?

No.

Eric the Wizard who turned knights into trees?

No.

Surely not Eric the hundred-year-old fire-breathing dragon that every knight was afraid of?

Yes, that Eric. Eric the Dragon.
He was huge.
He was dangerous.
He was always a bit angry.

"That would do the trick," said
Harry. "I'm sure I'll be made a
knight if I capture Eric!"
Oats neighed.

Harry packed a bag of things
he might need on his mission.
He packed his lunch. He packed
some oats. Oats needed to eat,
after all.

He packed some rope for tying up
Eric. He also borrowed his sister's
shield.

He might need it if Eric decided
to send a few flames of fire his way.

His sister wouldn't miss the shield.
Much.

Chapter Three

Harry and Oats set off to capture
the dragon.

The trouble was, Harry wasn't
exactly sure where Eric's cave
was.

He asked a man where Eric lived.
"Eric the Viking? Or Eric the
wizard?" asked the man.
"Eric the Dragon," said Harry.

The man looked shocked.
"Eric the Dragon? Are you
sure? He's usually a bit angry.
Especially before lunch."

"I'm going to capture him so that my father will make me a knight," said Harry.

"A very good plan," said the man.

He pointed to a nearby hill.
"Turn left at that old oak tree."
"Thank you, good sir," said
Harry.

Soon Harry spotted Eric's cave.
Harry stood behind his sister's
shield and shouted into the cave.

"Hey! Eric! Mister Dragon! Come
on out. I'm here to capture you!"
"Really? And how are you going
to do that?"
Harry spun around.

Behind Harry stood
a very large dragon.

Oats fainted.

Chapter Four

Harry was scared but knew he had to be brave. Brave like a knight.

"I am Harry the nearly-Knight. Come with me or I will have to tie you up."

Suddenly there was a loud,
gurgling noise. It was coming
from Eric. The dragon was
laughing!

Then he stopped.
"Ow," he said.

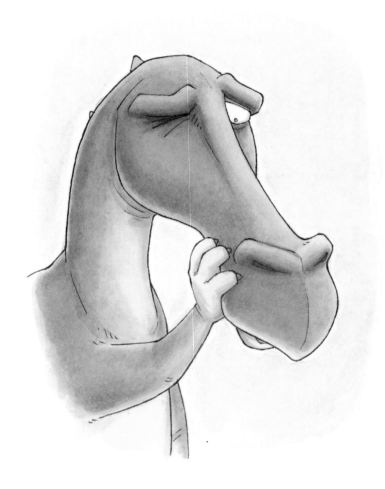

Harry looked at Oats.
Oats looked at Harry.

"What's up, Eric?" asked Harry.
"It's my tooth," said the dragon.
"It really hurts."

Eric opened his mouth. His teeth were big and sharp. One of them was black.

"Does it hurt?" asked Harry.
"Yes!" said Eric. "But I don't know
why I'm telling you. I'm about to
eat you."

Harry pulled out the rope.

"Maybe I can help you," he said.

"You? Help me?" said Eric.
He started laughing
again.

Then he pulled
a funny face.
"Owwwwww.
It really hurts."

"We can pull it out for you," said
Harry.
The dragon looked at Harry.
"Better out than in," said
Harry, smiling.

"Okay then," said the dragon.
"You can help me. Just this once."
Harry grinned.
"Before I eat you," said Eric.

Chapter Five

Harry tied the rope to the
dragon's bad tooth.

"Hold still," said Harry.
"This won't hurt a bit."

Oats tugged on the rope.

"Yes!" shouted Harry.

"Ooof," snuffled
Oats as he
fell down.

"Owwwwwwwwwwwww
wwwwww!"
cried Eric.

"Sorry about that,"
said Harry. "You'll feel
better now."

Eric rubbed his mouth.
"Mmmmnn.
It does feel better."

"I suppose you want me to let
you go," said Eric.
"No. I want you to let me capture
you," said Harry.

"Well, you have helped me," said Eric. "That tooth is why I've been so grumpy."

"So will you come back with me
and tell everyone how brave
I am?"

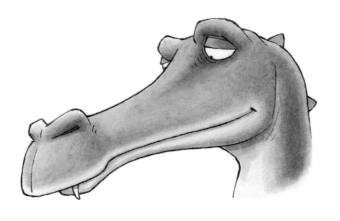

Eric smiled.
Well, maybe he did. It was hard
to tell.

"I can do better than that. We
can fly back to the castle," said
Eric. "That will look good."

It was the ride of Harry's life.

Chapter Six

Harry's dad put a sign on the door.

Harry was happy. His name was right at the top. He was the next knight-in-waiting.

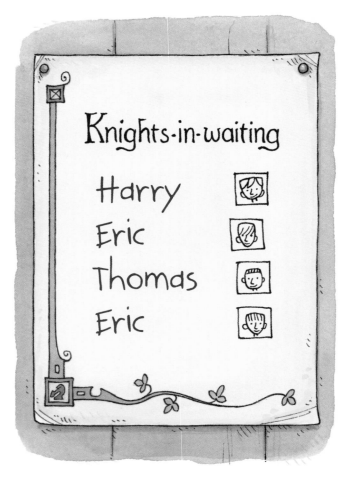

"Harry, I'm so proud of you,"
said his mum.

"You did good, squirt," said his
brother. "We've been trying to
stop Eric eating knights
for years."

"Where's my shield?" asked his sister.

"Just about to clean it now, dear sister," he said, ducking out of her way.

Harry sat down and picked up
his sister's shield. "Back to work,
Oats," he said, smiling.

"I'll be a knight soon, old boy.
And my dragon's tooth sword will
come in very handy!"

Oats the nearly-knightly horse
neighed loudly.

What are you going to read next?

Have more adventures with Horrid Henry,

and travel the world with

Miranda the Explorer.

Play clever tricks with Twit,

spend Mondays at Monster School,

and even brave The Dragon's Dentist . . .

Learn how love is just like a Woolly Hat,

dance under The Little Nut Tree,

take home Monstar, the best pet ever,

and have an extra-special Mr Monkey birthday party!

Enjoy all the Early Readers.